THE SOUND OF DANGER

D0727716

Titles in this series

JAMES STAGG

THE SOUND OF
DANGER

Collins
LONDON AND GLASGOW

First published 1967

Chapter One

THERE WAS FEAR sitting like an ugly gargoyle across the man's face. And a fearful, desperate anger—the anger of a man cornered like a rat. He crouched there in an angle of the rocks, the wind tearing at his coat, causing his over-long black hair to stream back from his forehead, and forcing his defiant, fear-ridden words back into his throat. To make himself heard he had to shout, and the anger and fear and the desperation turned the sound of his voice into a scream.

"You can't do this to me! What have I done?"

The four figures facing him in a menacing line, blocking his way to freedom, remained still and silent. And their very silence was a threat more ominous than words.

The man's voice battled against the gale again, and against the liquid thunder of the waves on the rocks and the rushing hiss as they withdrew to re-form in a mighty mass to attack the fortress of land once more.

5

"Why are you doing this? I have always done your dirty work! I've done nothing wrong!"

At the left of the group stood a figure swathed in a duffle coat with the hood pulled well forward. His face was further hidden behind a loosely bound scarf. He now made a small negative gesture with his right hand.

"You haven't done anything, George—yet. But you've been watched, and the word is that you're losing your nerve. That's dangerous, George—very dangerous. You're so close to me, George, that I can't afford the luxury of your losing your nerve. Especially as the other side have pin-pointed you."

It was a strange voice, with a throaty harshness about it that cut like a knife, and its owner appeared to have no trouble in making himself heard above the sounds of the wind and waves.

"But they can't have! I've played it cool! My cover hasn't been broken!"

"It has, George. They've broken your cover, and so you must go."

"Go? But where can I go? I'm not losing my nerve, I tell you! I've carried out my orders to the letter! Why must I go? *Where* can I go?" The words beat helplessly against the weather and uselessly against the four silent, implacable figures ranged rock-like before him.

The figure at the end of the line said, "Go? Who suggested you *go* anywhere? The word was figurative, George. It meant simply that you must cease to be."

"You're going to kill me!"

"That's right." The figure in the duffle coat spoke in a cold, objective tone, and turned slightly towards the others. He made a sudden sideways movement with his head.

The three other men moved towards the man called George.

"No! No!" The voice rose to a screech. "You can't! Not just like that! I've been loyal!"

He flung himself forward in panic-stricken desperation—trying to ram-rod his way through the three advancing figures. They reacted with the same swiftness. There was a struggling mass of bodies, and the sounds of feet scraping over the rocks and of hard breathing were lost in the sound the storm made.

The man who had made the sign of sentence of death remained impassive as the inevitable climax came. An arm was raised, and suddenly the hand, held flat, crashed down with vicious force on to the neck of the frantically struggling man. Abruptly he sagged, all movement ended.

The three men stepped back as the dufflecoated figure moved delicately forward a pace to peer down at the body of George lying on the spray-wet rocks.

"Good. You haven't killed him. He must have water in his lungs when they find him. Now drop him in the sea."

In the surging water, churned white where it fought the rocks, the falling body made no splash . . . no sound at all. . . .

Commander Royston Revel screwed his eyes into slits, and tried to see more clearly through the wind-driven rain. But visibility was cut to a few yards, despite the headlights of the car and the frantic working of the windscreen wipers. Ahead of him the night spread like a mass of saturated black velvet, soaking up the light beams and giving no sign of the way ahead.

An arm was raised and the hand crashed down . . .

The gale, the beat of the rain and the ever-present roar of the sea drowned even the hum of the engine, as Revel threaded his way along the coast road from St. Helier to the village of Gorey on the island of Jersey. Somewhere just on the other side of the village, up on the cliff top not far from Mont Orgueil Castle, there was a house, and at the house Revel had a rendezvous with a man named George Brent. The purpose of the rendezvous was to pay the man some money, and to persuade him to return with Revel to London.

He had a third task, one which only he and Makepeace knew about; it was a task only to be undertaken if Brent refused to return to London—or if efforts were made to prevent Brent accompanying him back to the capital.

The Department had known that Brent had turned double a long time ago; they had accepted it, and used him. Risks had been taken in letting him in on some quite dangerous information—dangerous to Britain if the other side were quick enough and clever enough to fit this with other information they might have gained through other sources.

Now the Department wanted to cash in on Brent; he had been given the leaked secrets to keep him at ease, to make him confident that his turning double had not been discovered. Now Makepeace wanted him back in London as a cog in a wheel that would turn swiftly and break up an organisation planted over the years in the United Kingdom by the other side. This organisation Makepeace firmly believed the United Kingdom could well do without.

The chief of Revel's Department had been laconic in his instructions to Revel; he always was. His habit of understatement had never been more pronounced than on this occasion, so that Revel knew that something really big was in the wind.

That was why Makepeace wanted George Brent back in London—or dead.

Revel knew no more than that. Makepeace was perhaps the only man who knew more—except for the Prime Minister. Makepeace sat in the offices above the jeweller's shop in a small, rather exclusive street off

Lansdowne Square in the West End; from there he pulled his hidden puppet strings controlling the movements of the men who guarded Britain's secrets, and who constantly lived in the sound and silence of danger.

Revel himself had been seconded from the Navy to the Department in the first place, because he was expert at handling a small boat. At that time Makepeace had wanted someone to run some guns to one of the newly-formed African states, as a diversionary movement to some larger global scheme that was afoot for the well-being and safety of Britain. The diversion had been such a success, due to Revel's initiative, that Makepeace had pulled a number of strings, other than his normal puppet strings, to have him transferred to a Department so secret that it had no name. It was referred to simply as " the Department " by the very few who knew of its existence.

And Revel admitted to himself that he had enjoyed every minute of the years he had spent with the Department. Death had sat on his shoulder more than once—a meaningless death that would never have been explained to the public. Loneliness in extreme danger he had experienced, too, when he knew that failure in a mission would bring a complete denial of the knowledge of his existence by Makepeace in private, and by Established Authority and the Government of Britain in public. So far he had been lucky. Death had left his shoulder with a laugh that implied that it could wait, and the loneliness had been scattered by success and a brief grin of welcome from Makepeace when Revel had returned from his assignment.

Roy Revel was a little under six feet tall, with a thick, chunky breadth of shoulder and depth of chest and an athlete's slim waist and hips. He carried not an ounce of surplus fat, was all bone and muscle, and was an expert in more than one form of unarmed mayhem. He had a good, lightning-quick brain, and was handsome in a craggy sort of way, with wiry brown hair and brown eyes that surveyed the world with an amused, wary understanding.

By the added force of the gale rather than by what his headlights showed him, Revel knew he was at the top of the climb. The castle would be on his right, and from there

—about another half-mile along the cliff-top road—he would find Boyard's House, where he had his rendezvous with the double agent, George Brent.

The road dipped again just past the castle, and the land went down to meet the sea; here there appeared to be a small bay for he could see the waves break in a line of white foam; moreover lights were moving about down there.

Revel was suddenly aware of a uniformed man waving a torch, picked out in the head-lights. Revel stopped the car by the island policeman, who bent to speak in at the wound-down side window of the car.

"We could do with some help down there, sir. Body washed ashore. Would you mind giving us a hand? It's not a pleasant . . ."

"I'm not too squeamish, officer. Be glad to help."

The wind lifted Revel's hat from his head as soon as he stood out from the protection of the car, and flung it viciously into the rain-lashed darkness. Revel shrugged and followed the policeman, who was making heavy work of walking down the steep slope and rough ground, treading in the pool of light which dripped from the torch he held in his hand.

On the beach there was another policeman, and a boy of about fifteen, waterproofed from head to foot in oilskins. There was also a shapeless mass of saturated clothing lying on the shingle where it had been dragged clear of the clawing fingers of the waves.

The policeman on the beach looked up as they approached. The other said, "This gentleman has kindly consented to help," in the stilted way of a constable giving evidence in the Magistrates' Court.

"Very good of you, sir." The beach policeman turned to the oilskinned boy. "Right, John. You get on back home now. Your Mum and Dad will wonder what on earth's happened to you. You've done a good job."

In the spill-light from the torches Revel saw the boy grin; then he turned, picked up some fishing tackle lying on the beach, and made his way up towards the road.

"Letting a boy out fishing this time of

night and in this weather," said the policeman who had stopped Revel. "Still, if he hadn't been here fishing, the body could have been washed up to-night and washed out again by the dawn's tide, and we might never have found it. Now, sir, if you'll be good enough to take one corner at the head . . . Harry—can you manage the other? I'll take the feet."

The body had been laid on one of the policemen's capes. For the first time Revel saw the face in the beam of a torch. He bent to take hold of the corner indicated by the policeman, but he gave no sign that his journey from London to the Channel Islands had been wasted; he also gave no sign that he knew the drowned man as George Brent.

Before they lifted him, one of the policemen said, "Don't happen to know him, do you, sir?"

Revel shook his head. "Never saw him before in my life."

The other policeman said, "I told you, Harry. I'm almost sure it's that chap who moved into Boyard's a couple of months ago. Now come on—let's get him up to the car and back to St. Helier. We'll find out who he is soon enough."

The man standing at the window of Boyard's House turned away, drew the curtains to cover the window, and said, " Right."

Lights suddenly blazed in the darkened room, and the man moved from the window. On an occasional table he put a pair of binoculars to which was attached a small, square, box-like fitting.

He was tall—immensely tall—with a frame to match his height. He was almost bald, but his face and neck were unlined. He wore a placid expression on his heavy, roundish face, about which there was nothing remarkable until the eyes were noticed. The irises were of different colours—one being a pale, cold blue, the other a flecked green. His hands were large, the fingers thick, and when he moved he gave the impression of bull-like strength.

Beside him the two other men in the room were insignificant, and Damien Flek treated them as if that were indeed his opinion of them. He spoke with a cold arrogance in a harsh, knife-edged voice.

"The advantages of this infra-red attachment to the binoculars are legion," he said. "We know that George's body has been discovered—quite by chance in the vicinity of this house. And by letting us see his face as if by the light of day, we know that our information was right, that Revel had been given the task of taking George to London."

Flek smiled, and when he did, his face became softened and benign. He looked at the other two men in turn, drenching them in his smile.

"You, Lazlo." The man rose from the chair in which he had been lounging. He was above middle height, but thin, with long tapering fingers, a long tapering nose and a long tapering chin. "And you, Saul." The other man rose to his feet; his size matched that of his companion, but he was more thickly built; he had a square face, with the high cheek bones of the Slav and his eyes were icy-blue and without warmth.

"You will both now prepare to receive Mr. Revel. We all know what we are to do with him, don't we?"

Lazlo nodded, his nods tapering away like

the rest of him. Saul smiled, but it was just a stretching of the thin lips, and it switched off with the abruptness with which he had recently switched on the lights in the room at Flek's command.

"We all know, don't we, that Revel is not to be allowed to leave this island? And that he will never see England through his own eyes at any rate, again—don't we?"

The doorbell rang. Flek's benign smile drenched Lazlo and Saul afresh. "There— our guest has arrived. Go and let him in, Lazlo. Show him in here."

As Lazlo left the room, Flek seated himself behind an ornate mahogany desk, opened the top right-hand drawer, and checked that the silencer was properly fitted to the gun that lay there.

Chapter Two

THE HOUSE standing with its head into the wind on the top of the cliff, looked dark and empty, without a heart. The sound of Revel's feet on the tarmac path leading from the road to the front door was lost in the noise of the beating rain and driving wind.

The lights of the ambulance coming out from St. Helier towards them had been like a glowing island of yellow, as Revel left the two policemen waiting at the side of the road with their dead-weight burden. He had gone to his car, and had driven up the hill which rose from the dip of the bay towards the point where the gaunt house stood. Some yards beyond the house he had stopped the car and walked back.

It was unlikely that George Brent had left in Boyard's House anything that would be of use to the Department—he was too old a hand for that—but just in case the old hand had become careless, Revel would have to search the house. Perhaps Brent had left some sort of household behind; if so, Revel would need to be aware of their strength, numbers, dispositions and, if he were lucky, any knowledge they had of Brent's activities. The quickest way to find out if there was anybody in the house was to ring at the front door. If there was no reply, he would be able to break in, and take a chance on a cagey associate of Brent's lurking in the dark, or a frightened but innocent housekeeper hiding her head under the bedclothes.

As he had walked along the garden path towards the door of the house, he had been guided in the darkness by the small yellow eye of light that pin-pointed the bell-push. Now he put forward the stiff index finger of his left hand, and poked it in the unwinking yellow eye.

A light was switched on in the hall behind the glass-fronted door almost immediately, and a bulky shadow moved like an animated silhouette on the glass, looming larger as it came towards him. The door opened and the silhouette became a substantial, unsmiling man with high cheek-bones and cold eyes, who listened without an expression on his face as Revel told his hastily contrived cover-story of a broken-down car. Finally he asked if he could use the telephone to get on to a garage in St. Helier?

The thickly-built man said nothing, but stepped aside, motioning Revel to step inside. Revel was led along a short passageway and shown into a brightly lit room. He walked warily because of the immediate and silent acceptance with which he had been welcomed into the house; it was almost as if he had been expected.

He had never before seen the immensely tall, giant-built, bald man who rose from behind a desk facing the doorway, to assure him that of course he could use the telephone. First, however, he invited him to sit down and take a drink to reinforce himself against the weather?

The strangely coloured eyes flicked slightly towards Saul, standing a little behind Revel. Then Flek extended a large, fleshy hand towards a low-backed arm-chair which faced the desk at an angle, its back towards the door.

"My dear sir, please—sit down. I heard you tell my man your predicament as I sat here. Do sit down. And Saul will get you a drink. What will it be? Whisky? It's a

A thickly-built man stood in the door-way . . .

dreadful night outside." He spoke well, his voice having a deep, rich timbre as well as the slightest of accents which Revel found hard to place. There was a tinge of harsh Slavonic, which in certain words became strangely softened by a Latin influence.

"It's very good of you." Revel sat down.

"Not at all. I'd offer you the hospitality of a bed for the night—but it is not my house." The big man sat down, and gestured with a gentle waving movement of his left hand. "It belongs to my cousin, who, unfortunately, is away on the mainland on business."

The large, round face beneath the shiny, stubbly pate, was benign; the lips smiled and the smile actually touched the differently coloured eyes which looked at Revel with a disarming frankness and friendliness.

"It's very good of you," said Revel again, "to let me come in and drench your carpet with rainwater."

The big man shook his head. "It is not my carpet, and I am sure my cousin would think it of little account." He raised his head fractionally, flicking his eyes momentarily towards the door behind Revel. "Saul is taking a long time getting your drink, but there, he is a little slow to be sure—slow, but sure." His smile drenched Revel again. "My name, incidentally is Flek—Damien Flek."

He went on talking, his deep voice lulling the very air of the room into a sort of drowsiness. But Revel did not hear the words that were spoken after the big man had repeated his name; for the glass door of the elegant book-case behind Flek was open a few inches and because of the angle at which it stood, the door behind Revel was reflected in the glass. The man called Saul had come through that door and was now moving stealthily towards Revel from behind, his right hand held up, the fingers and palm held stiff and flat.

Revel tensed himself. He had been expecting something like this ever since he entered the house. His mind started to measure distances with the swiftness of a computer at work. . . . The karate blow would come swinging down at the back of his neck from the right. . . . So he must move with the direction of the blow. That was good because it would keep a large portion of the desk between him and the man sitting behind it, and the cover would give him enough time to pull his automatic from its shoulder-holster. If the impetus of the blow carried Saul in the direction in which Revel would throw himself, that was good too, because Revel could use his feet as well as his fists. . . . His muscles became taut, his right hand was slowly beginning to move towards the inside of his jacket. He must move. . . .

Suddenly, the soporific tones of Flek's voice were silenced as the shrilling of the electric door-bell exploded into the room.

Flek raised his eyes momentarily from Revel's face to that of Saul. "Ah Saul," he said, still in the gentle voice he had been using. "We are having a busy night. You had better see who it is."

In the glass door, Revel saw the man's hand drop to his side as he swung round to go to the door; he gave no sign that he was aware of the intended attack. Flek sat back easily in his chair, his smile broadening at Revel and outwardly not at all put out by the interruption.

Saul returned after a few moments, accompanied by the policeman who had stopped Revel on the road earlier.

The huge figure of Flek, lounging back in the chair behind the desk, dominated the room. The policeman's eyes went to him at once.

"Sorry to bother you at this time of night, sir. Are you the owner of this house?"

Flek's smile seemed to be fixed to his lips. "This gentleman made the same mistake." For the first time the policeman noticed Revel.

"Oh, hello, sir," he said, surprised. Revel nodded.

Flek said, "The house belongs to my cousin, Mr. Brent."

"Oh." The policeman rubbed his chin thoughtfully. "There has been a bit of a nasty accident, sir. A man's body has just been washed up in the bay below the house. We had an idea it might be . . . er . . . Mr. Brent."

"I should think that most unlikely, officer. You see, my cousin is on the mainland—a business visit."

The policeman still did not appear to be happy. "I wonder. . . . We wouldn't have bothered you, sir . . . we thought the house was empty. No lights or movement . . . that's why we thought it *might* be Mr. Brent. And then, just as the ambulance was about to take the body back to St. Helier, we saw a light come on in the house. I thought I'd just come on up and check."

"Very praiseworthy of you, officer. Especially in this weather, but . . ."

"Perhaps you wouldn't mind—just to make sure—coming into St. Helier in the morning, sir. Just to establish that the dead man is not your cousin?" Now the policeman spoke in his stilted courtroom manner.

"But of course. If one can definitely close an avenue of inquiry to save the police wasting their time. . . . Will ten o'clock be early enough?"

"Thank you, sir. Well, I'll be off. Sorry to have troubled you."

Revel was on his feet before the policeman had finished turning for the door. "I'll not . . . er . . . trouble you any further, either, Mr. Flek. The officer will be able to help me, I'm sure."

Flek gave no indication of his feelings.

The smile stayed clamped to his lips, and he rose slowly from his chair. "What a pity Saul was so long with that drink.... You're sure you won't stay....?"

Revel smiled and shook his head. From the doorway the policeman watched him with a question on his face. He put it into words as Revel approached him. "What can I do for you, sir?"

Roy Revel said, "Good-night, Mr. Flek. Thank you for your offer of help—and for all you were going to do for me."

He walked purposefully past the constable towards the front door, which Saul opened and held against the gale. Heavy-footed, the policeman followed. Outside, on the wind-swept, rain-drenched road, Revel grinned at the officer, the rain driving into his face.

"I'm trying to get to St. Peter's airport, officer. I seem to have taken the wrong road altogether. I stopped at the first house I saw to ask the way."

"Pity you didn't mention it when I stopped you, sir. I could have saved you the trouble. Anyway, I shouldn't think there'd be any planes taking off from there to-night in this weather. A pity you didn't mention it when I stopped you." He shook his head at the pity of it all.

" I had no inkling I was on the wrong road, then."

The policeman looked at him as if he was a half-wit. " On this road you never *would* have got to St. Peter's, sir. Not unless you drove all the way round the island. Now, the best thing for you to do, is to turn round and get back to Gorey—that's the village at the bottom of the hill below the castle. There's a sign post there. Just follow that."

Revel patiently listened to the further detailed instructions for which he had no use, thanked the officer, and watched the man climb on to his cycle and wobble off down the hill into the wind and rain. Then he moved swiftly to his car and drove on for about a mile without turning, before he stopped. He took a cigarette lighter from his pocket, pulled out a minute aerial from the top, held the small oblong case close to his mouth and said, " Roland calling Oliver. Roland calling Oliver." Monotonously he repeated the call nearly a dozen times before the lace-like side of the lighter emitted the sound of an answering voice. "This had better be good. I was asleep."

Revel smiled grimly to himself. He was tuned in to the personal wave-length of Makepeace, who, under normal conditions, was a seven-hours'-sleep-a-night man. And he slept heavily.

"The goods, unfortunately, have already been despatched. I believe the despatcher is a man who calls himself Flek. Huge, Friar Tuck-like character, with two differently coloured eyes. I don't know him. Do you? He also tried to despatch our representative."

There was silence for a few moments, then the lace-work spoke again. "Voltaire had one of his characters say that all is for the best in this best of all possible worlds. We've lost a minnow and found a whale. Get this man. The other goods were not worth a wooden penny by comparison. You are to take all steps—even your last if necessary—to eliminate the subject. It is vital, vital, vital. Understood?"

"Understood. Anything more?"

"What else do you want? A written

order? You'll be lucky! Now get off my wave-length. I want to go to sleep."

Revel pushed down the small aerial; the minute, grim smile returned to his lips. He knew Makepeace would sleep no more that night. Vital, vital, vital—this was the highest category of urgency in the Department, where urgency was a commonplace state. It was never used except in matters of extreme national danger. Mr. Flek must be a very big fish indeed; he must also be a very dangerous fish indeed. Revel had received his orders to execute this danger to the nation —even if it meant losing his own life to accomplish it.

And one way or another it had to be done now.

Chapter Three

REVEL drove the car back to a spot which he judged to be a quarter of a mile from the house. Here on the cliff top, with the wind dragging at every movable thing, and with the roaring, hissing waves hammering at the rocks below, he left the car. He was already so wet that another drenching would make no difference; he knew the automatic in his shoulder holster would be dry, and just now, that was all that mattered. He walked through the sodden, wind-tortured grass on the top of the cliff, towards the side of the house.

The dark shadow of the square, rugged shape of Boyard's House loomed suddenly in front of him behind the shimmering curtain of rain. There were no lights showing from it now. Peering at the dark mass, Revel failed to see the low stone wall surrounding the garden in which the house stood. His knees bumped it, and the top of it, stomach high, brought a grunt of shock from him. He felt for the pencil-slim torch in his inside jacket pocket, and for the other tools of his trade which helped him to open windows, safes and doors, and other such obstacles. He carried these small metal tools on a ring as other men carried keys, and they were all present and correct. He put his hands on the top of the wall, peered over to see what sort of landing he would make, and vaulted over, his feet sinking in the mud of a long unattended flower bed.

Just then, a roar, louder than the buffeting wind, rode over the noise of the weather. It came from the bottom of the cliff, below the point where the sloping garden of the house ended abruptly.

The roar increased, died away and returned again suddenly. Revel moved towards the lower end of the garden as swiftly as his night blindness and the unknown quantity of the contours of the garden would allow. He found himself standing at the top of some steps cut into the side of the cliff. They led steeply down to a small cove where the water frothed white, as the defiant rocks broke up attack after attack by the endless waves.

Suddenly, from the black, right-hand side

Suddenly a large and powerful motor launch emerged.

of the cliffs, it seemed, a large and powerful motor launch emerged, its shape thrown into relief by the angry white water. It carried no navigation lights, and in the storm-riven darkness Revel could not see clearly; but he thought he saw the figures of three men in the powerful launch. The vessel sliced into the incoming white-topped waves, its engines roaring mockingly at the mighty strength of the enemy it was confronting. It moved out of the small cove, rising on the white-caps and sinking into the troughs, but always moving powerfully away from the land, until its shape was lost in the wet blackness of the night.

Revel turned towards the house. Its silent shape crouched on the high cliff, its very attitude appearing to taunt Revel because his victim had got away.

A ground-floor window at the rear of the house was easily opened and Roy stepped over the sill, the thin beam of his torch picking out the pots and pans, the stove and table of a kitchen. He stood there, just inside the window, water dripping from him, and listened. The wind whined and moaned now, and the gusting rain hammered a million small blows on the windows, but within the house there was an empty stillness.

Revel moved stealthily towards the door, his mind working, his muscles alert. Flek knew him, knew what he had come to do, and had arranged a reception for him. The arrival of the policeman had prevented the mayhem he had intended, and he knew that Revel would come back, perhaps with reinforcements. And it seemed that Damien Flek was so keen to keep his freedom, that the thought of escape had over-ridden any other plans he might have had. In short, he had run for it. Not because he might have been responsible for Brent's death and was afraid to face the consequences: the chances were that it could never have been proved that Flek was Brent's killer, anyway. So— why?

And what was Flek's connection with Brent—apart from his being on the other side, and in all likelihood being Brent's contact with them? Did Brent's death mean that they had broken his double cover? It was more than likely. But there was a great deal more to Flek than just being a hatchet man for the other side. Makepeace had never used the National Emergency call in his dealings with Revel before.

Roy told himself to stop wondering; his job was to make Flek die. But now, first, he had to find Flek. The man's departure had been hurried. Was it possible for him to have known of the death call that had gone out for him? Perhaps there was just a chance that the house, or something in it, might disclose a wisp of information that would put Revel on his trail.

Revel discovered the room he had been in only recently, and went through the desk behind which Flek had been seated. It yielded nothing; the room yielded nothing, although Roy searched it with the ruthless thoroughness which was one of the first fundamentals in the training of men selected to work for the Department.

Guided by the long, thin, pointing finger of his torch, he found another room lined with bookshelves which reached from the floor to the ceiling. In the room was a short step-ladder, two easy-chairs, a table at which three hard-seated, upright chairs were placed, and a globe of the world. Revel sighed as the small spotlight picked out the hundreds of books lining the walls; if he followed his teaching, every one of these volumes would have to be taken down and inspected. . . . It was ridiculous. . . . But where *would* Flek have flown to? Where *could* he fly to on a night such as this? The launch Revel had seen and heard was obviously powerful, obviously very seaworthy; but even a launch of such power and sturdiness would have its limitations in the rough seas which were hammering at the island.

The nearest point on the coast of France was only fifteen miles away. . . . If Flek was really saying good-bye to Jersey, if his dangerous night sea trip was not just a feint, or if he were not making for one of the other islands, the nearby coast of France was . . .

The slightest of sounds, which had nothing to do with the roar and rush of weather outside, made him turn suddenly, the beam of his torch swinging with him. The moving finger of light picked out the figure of a man coming towards him at a jump—the violent culmination of a stealthy approach.

A heavy-headed torch, held in the man's right hand, came crashing down towards Revel's head; it missed his skull and landed with an arm-numbing agony on his shoulder, —Revel's reflexes were in good order. He had barely time to move his head the few inches to avoid the blow, but he had managed it. And then, almost simultaneously with the torch landing so forcefully on his shoulder, the man's whole body crashed into him. Revel's torch went flying from his hand as they both fell to the floor.

His attacker had the arms and legs of an octopus—long and with steel-wire strength. They wrapped themselves round Revel with the force and suddenness of a taut hawser snapping under undue weight, and whipping back in a lethal coil.

But as they fell, with the man's arms already trying to stop any freedom of movement that might be left to him, Revel had flung out his right arm. As they hit the floor, this was the only limb he possessed which had not been imprisoned. He straightened his hand so that the fingers and palms were as stiff as a board, then twisting his wrist unnaturally so that the palm was uppermost, he brought his arm inwards, in as powerful a chopping movement as he could manage.

It was a blind blow, attempted in a split second; it was not direct on target as he had hoped, but it sliced home near enough—on the side of the man's neck, forcing a grunt from him, and hammering his forehead on to Revel's teeth.

The man's grip loosened momentarily with the shock of the unexpected pain, and in that split second Revel was able to bring his knee up into the man's stomach. In the same powerful movement, he kicked upwards and the slim, wiry body went with the kick. The clawing fingers scratched past Revel's face as the attacker was flung up into the blackness of the room. Revel twisted away from the spot on which he had been lying. A moment later the body came down again to land with an unpleasant thud on the carpeted floorboards.

The white smudge of the man's face was uppermost, and Revel hammered his fist into the middle of the target. The head hit the floor again, and the body went limp.

Revel pushed himself up from his knees, and blundered across the room, feeling his way along the wall until he came to the light switch. He had no qualms now about flooding the house with light. If there had been anyone else in the building, the noise of the fight would have brought them running.

The light seered into his eyes for a few moments until they became accustomed to the brightness. He picked up his torch and found it was still working—it was built to withstand greater shocks than merely being flung from his hand. Then he turned to the man on the floor; he was lying at full stretch, with blood on his thin-featured face, his abnormally long arms flung out at right angles to his body. This was not the man who had been about to attack him on his first visit to the house. . . . So—Flek had other birds in his gilded cage. . . .

Revel threw away some flowers from a vase he found on a small table in the hall just outside the room, and flung the stale water in the man's face. Then he took his automatic from his pocket in a leisurely movement, seated himself on the edge of the table, and with one leg gently swinging, waited for the thin man to come round.

This took two minutes, by which time he was half-sitting on the floor, leaning back on his elbow, his light blue eyes still glazed. His face wore a stupid, unknowing expression, as his scattered wits ran around inside his head, trying to collect themselves.

Revel dangled his automatic in front of the man's eyes, drawing them up to his own face. Gradually the blankness left the light blue eyes as they focused on Revel.

"You should always," said Revel, his leg still swinging gently, "knock before you enter a room. You never know who you might run into."

He unhitched himself from the edge of the table, bent suddenly, and with his automatic still in his right hand, grabbed the man by the lapels of his jacket, heaved him up, and then sent him flying backwards into one of the arm-chairs. The chair ran back on its runners with some force, until it fetched up against one of the bookcases, bringing down from the upper shelves a shower of books which landed without malice on and around the head of the thin man.

Revel stood in front of him as he lolled back, bereft of fight or the will to fight.

"Now," said Revel in a quiet conversational tone, " one way or another you are going to tell me where our mutual friend, Damien Flek, is heading for."

He smiled down at the man, and lifted him by the knot of his tie some twelve inches from the chair, before throwing him down into it again.

" You are going to tell me exactly what I want to know, and you have a choice as to the manner in which you give me the information. You can do it conversationally, or you can be stubborn and suffer a very, very great deal of pain. But you are going to tell me —and you are going to tell me the truth."

The man's bruised lips twisted into a strange smile—a smile that should have warned Revel, but which somehow, in the urgency of the situation, did not.

The thin man said, " Pain administered in cold blood I never could stand. Especially when administered to me. I'll tell you what you want to know."

Chapter Four

THE SIX-SEATER charter aircraft, piloted by
a keen young type who used the Royal Air
Force slang of twenty years before, deposited
Revel near the control tower of the airfield
at St. Malo. The French Customs, happy
for any visitor and his money, gave him but
a cursory glance.

A down-at-the-springs Citroën taxi jarred
him into the town itself, to a branch of
Crédit Lyonnais. Here he collected some
money arranged for him by the Department
earlier that day, following his second radio
talk with Headquarters.

The thin man had given him the name of
a villa—*Maison Bleu*—overlooking the sea
some three miles along the coast from St.
Malo. This was, he told Revel, where Flek
had been making for.

A heavy-eyed police sergeant at St. Helier,
had somewhat dazedly opened a cell door
to accommodate Revel's prisoner, and Makepeace, on the radio, had repeated the

National Emergency call—"vital, vital, vital."

"If you have to follow him to the ends of the world, get that man," Makepeace had told him. "If you have to die in the attempt, then die. But make sure Flek is dead first."

The words sounded callous, and Revel knew that Makepeace meant every one of them. He also knew that should the end come for him in this assignment, Makepeace would mourn him very deeply and very sincerely. And then he would select his next best man, and send him out to complete the task he had set Revel—or die in the attempt. For the work in which the Department was concerned Makepeace did not reckon the cost in individual lives when the safety and very life of the whole nation was largely in his keeping.

Revel's eyes were gritty from lack of sleep as he signed the form at the garage in St. Malo from which he hired a car—a not entirely new Mercedes.

He took the coast road leading to Paramé. *Maison Bleu* stood on its own, on the land-

ward side of the road which hugged the coast.
It was a pleasant house, with large picture
windows, which would have given glorious
wide views of the sea—had they not been
shuttered. There was a terraced garden that
sloped gently down from the rise on which
the house was built to the large, double
wrought-iron gates opening on to the road.
There was an old man in blue knee-length
overalls and baggy trousers working with a
hoe at one of the flower beds. The house
looked as if it had not yet been opened for
the holiday season by its owners. The paint
of the woodwork and of the delicate shutters
over the windows, like decorative patches
over the eyes of the house, was egg-shell blue.

Revel drove past the place and stopped
nearly a mile farther on, after the bend in
the road and a gently rising hill had hidden
him from view of the house. He walked
back over the hill, approaching the building
from the tilled fields away from the sea.
Viewed from the rear, the house appeared as
empty as it did from the front.

He walked back to the road and boldly
passed through the wrought-iron gates. The

old gardener leaned on his hoe, and looked up.

Revel smiled. "I'm looking for the owner," he said.

The old man spat into a bed of rose bushes nearby. "Then m'sieur is very unlucky," he answered. "For M'sieur Dumont left but some thirty minutes ago."

The old man's patois made it a little difficult for Revel to understand what he was saying. "*Comment?*"

Patiently the gardener repeated what he had said, slowly, as if he were talking to a child.

Revel slapped his thigh in a show of disappointment. "You wouldn't know by any chance where I might find him?"

Once again the old man spat at the rose bed; he seemed to dislike it. "Lyons."

"Lyons!" Revel's voice had a note of disbelief in it. He changed his tone. "M. Dumont—he is a very large man, with a round, bald head and a large round face?"

Now the gardener was sure he was confronted by an imbecile. "Of course. Who else would it be?"

" And you're sure he is going to Lyons?"

Revel took a hundred franc note from his pocket and played with it. The old man stopped himself from spitting at the roses for a third time, eyeing the money with a more lively interest than he had yet shown.

" He told you he was going to Lyons, eh?"

" Of course he didn't. But I heard him tell that big Pole who drives him—Saul they call him—to make sure that the car didn't break down between here and Lyons. Look," the old man went on, enchanted by the sight of the money, " M. Dumont drove here this morning, not long after I arrived for work. He went into the house, was inside for about fifteen minutes, and when he came out he was carrying a lot of papers. As he and the Pole walked out of the door of the house to the car, I heard him say that bit about the car not breaking down between here and Lyons. It was important. Then they got in and drove away."

" Didn't he exchange a word with you?"

" Why should he? Except to say 'Good morning'. And to pay me. He employs me in the spring and summer to keep the garden tidy—not as a conversationalist."

"And he spoke in French?"

"And if he didn't speak in French, what language should he have spoken in?" The old man was now more than ever sure he was dealing with an idiot, but the hundred franc note held loosely in Revel's hands was a sight to temper any outright rudeness.

"What sort of a car has he got?"

"I haven't seen the one he came here to-day in, before. Usually he drives a Citroën, but this one was one of those big German cars—a Mercedes. It's new and white."

Revel held out the note. "You've been very helpful."

The old man wiped his hands on the seat of his trousers, letting the hoe fall unheeded to the ground. He took the note reverently from Revel, and slid it into a pocket in the seat of his baggy trousers.

"It hurts your eyes to look at it," he said as Revel walked back to the wrought-iron gates. And Revel knew he was referring to the white Mercedes and not to the hundred franc note.

Back at the car he sat behind the wheel, pondering on what he had learnt. It was almost too good to be true. At their first meeting Flek had spoken English almost without an accent; he spoke French well enough to make a native of the country believe it was his mother tongue. Here, he went by a French name. If the old man was working anywhere near the spot at which Revel had been talking to him, Flek must have spoken very loudly for the old man to hear. And for a man who wanted to hide himself, a large, new, white Mercedes was hardly the least conspicuous of cars.

Revel sat looking at nothing, and he tapped his teeth with his right thumbnail. Flek was not just running blindly to escape—he was running, and laying a trail as he went, and not too cleverly, either. That was assuming he wanted Revel to follow without knowing that the trail was being laid for him.

But that was just it! Flek didn't care whether Revel followed the trail without knowing he was meant to or not. So long as he followed. This meant that Flek must somehow *know* that Revel would dog his footsteps no matter where he went, and it meant, too, that Flek wanted to be sure that Revel was able to follow him without any difficulty. Even the man left behind at Boyard's House had been left there, not to do irreparable damage to Revel, but to make sure that he started off on the chase in the right direction.

Somewhere along the line, therefore, a trap was being laid for him. Revel grinned wolfishly; the only things about which Flek would make sure that Revel received no information, would be the nature of the trap, and where and when it would be sprung.

This was cat and mouse with a vengeance —or rather fox and hounds. . . . the cunning fox leading the eager hounds to the edge of a precipice, and watching them—from a hide-out nearby—tumble over it in their frantic desire to get to their quarry and tear him to pieces.

Revel started the engine, slid the gear lever into first, and did a U-turn from a standing start in the lay-by in which he had halted. He headed back for St. Malo. His abrupt movement and turn scattered three oncoming cars, the white-faced drivers of which took immediate and frantic evasive action.

"Hounds, gentlemen, please!" said Revel

softly as he continued to hog the right of way, leaving the three drivers to curse him loud and long—once they had swallowed their hearts which had suddenly risen into their mouths.

A smile sat on Revel's lips all the way on the short drive back to St. Malo.

Chapter Five

REVEL drove the newer Mercedes model he had hired from the same garage, into one of the lock-ups attached to the small hotel where he had booked a room. He looked at his wrist watch and grinned. It was an hour since he had arrived back in St. Malo from *Maison Bleu*. He sighed with satisfaction as he thought of the comfortable bed awaiting him; four or five hours' sleep would take the grittiness from his eyes for another forty-eight hours, perhaps. While he was asleep, the Department would be making arrangements to give his hired car international clearance, in the event of the chase taking him beyond Lyons and the frontiers of France.

It gave him a pleasant feeling to be able to control at least this part of the hunt after Flek's long solo on the hunting horn. If the man was making sure that Revel would follow him into a trap he could kick his heels for a few hours longer while the hound caught up on some sleep. It was pleasant to know that the quarry would make sure his scent remained alive and clear for the hunter to follow.

The wolfish smile that had played about Revel's lips so frequently during the past hour, gave way to one of feline, tigerish satisfaction as he put his head on the pillow, and pulled the sheet up over his head, to dim still further the grey light filtering through the closed shutters.

It was three o'clock in the afternoon when he woke up—on schedule. He took a shower, put on a clean shirt, changed his suit, settled his bill, and then found a restaurant which served him with a late lunch. By the time he was driving out of St. Malo on a south-east course, it was a little after five o'clock, with the sun still high, and not a cloud in the sky.

In the early hours of the following morning he was at Le Mans; by mid-day he was at Orléans, where he shaved and showered, and had lunch in a hotel on the banks of the Loire. At various points along the route he had asked after a white Mercedes, but only once, at a garage where it had stopped for petrol, did he hear news of it. The very silence of the Mercedes' passing was the sound of danger, and Revel had the feeling that from now on, every mile he covered on the way to Lyons, would be more dangerous than the last.

By two o'clock he was driving along the road which followed the Loire valley, more than ever alert for the smallest sign of danger. Where would Flek strike? And how? And why all this trailing across France? Revel knew why *he* was trailing across France—he had to eliminate Flek. But what was Flek's purpose in drawing him across the country? Perhaps it didn't matter. On the other hand, perhaps if he knew Flek's purpose, it might give him a lead as to how, when and where he would be attacked.

But none of these questions could be answered until he made contact with Flek. And even then there might be no time to ask them.

Anyway, Lyons was the key. Flek wanted Revel in Lyons. There were a number of alternative routes to Lyons, any one of which Revel could have taken, and Flek couldn't possibly cover them all to prepare a trap for him to drive into. So it was in Lyons where he would face most danger.

At Nevers he had an evening meal and made a telephone call to Lyons—to the Hotel Royal in the Place Bellecour, and reserved a room. He told them he expected to arrive in the small hours of the morning.

In the dark hours, at Moulins, he took the road to Mâcon instead of crossing the mountains. From Mâcon he would be able to follow the road due south as it partnered the River Saône along its valley to Lyons— an easier route.

Revel arrived at the Hotel Royal shortly after three o'clock in the morning. One of the night porters took the car to the hotel garage and Revel took himself to bed. He was where Flek wanted him to be. Now it was up to Flek. The next few hours might see the death of one or the other of them— but he proposed not to lose any sleep over it.

It was the sound of the catch of the door

clicking crisply back into place that disturbed him just over an hour later, and the sudden glare of the lights in the room being switched on that woke him a few moments after. Almost at the same time as the lights blazed on, he was sitting up in bed, his hand under the pillow grasping at the butt of his automatic.

Then he saw the man standing at the foot of the bed, and looked directly into the single, hollow eye-socket of a heavy Service revolver fitted with a silencer. It was trained very accurately between Revel's eyes.

The man behind the gun was of medium height, but Revel had never seen so wide a pair of shoulders or such a depth of chest beneath so large a head. The man was dark, with crisp crinkly hair and eyes of deep brown, hot now with excitement.

He said nothing, but made signs with his free hand for Revel to dress. He made a further sign which Revel took to mean that when he removed his hand from underneath the pillow it had better be empty.

Revel made sure that it was, swung himself out of bed, and made for his clothes.

He was brought up short by a belligerent gesture from the gun.

The mute smiled thinly, and signalled to Revel to stay where he was. Then, keeping his eye on Revel, the silent gunman went through each pocket of each garment and felt every lining, removing anything he found, before tossing the articles of clothing to Revel one by one.

Revel lifted his right eyebrow in a question. "No shower? Not even a clean tooth. My dentist won't like that. Every morning, he says, and when you go to bed—as well as other times during the day. In fact, he would like me to give up my job and spend my whole time cleaning my teeth."

The mute's eyes hardened; he shook his head angrily and gestured for Revel to hurry.

"Can I use the mirror to tie my tie? I've never learned to knot it without a mirror."

The gun gestured towards the mirror on the dressing-table. Revel smiled his thanks and moved towards it, the gun and the man following him. The gun prodded him in the back once or twice indicating very clearly to Revel that the mute was getting impatient with him.

He stood in front of the mirror near the rug covering part of the carpet in the centre of the room—and dropped his tie.

He bent slowly to pick it up. His fingers touched the tie, and then moved like lightning to the edge of the rug, grasping it firmly. In the same movement he heaved himself upright, bringing the rug with him. The gunman's feet shot from under him and he fell backwards. A bullet from his silenced gun plunked into the ceiling. Revel pivoted on one foot, bringing the other round in a quick kick that connected with the gunman's wrist as he hit the floor.

The gun sliced across the room and smashed into the long mirror in the wardrobe door.

"Your seven years' bad luck starts right now," said Revel as he crashed down on to the fallen man. The mute gave a gasping, explosive grunt as the air was steam-hammered from his body, and the hot, brown eyes were no longer excited, but afraid.

He clawed at Revel's eyes with his undamaged hand, and Revel brought his fist swinging at an angle to the side of the man's jaw. The eyes rolled up to the top of his

He heaved himself upright, bringing the rug with him.

head, the big head lolled sideways, the jaw sagged.

Outside in the corridor there were the sounds of running footsteps and excited voices. Revel, ignoring the noise, went through the mute's pockets quickly, transferring their contents to his own, save for some money, some keys and six or seven dog-eared and strangely domestic photographs of a family group.

By the time the excited knocking had reached a climax, Revel was moving towards the door, to unbolt it, his own automatic and the gun with the silencer safely in his pocket. His tie, too, was neatly knotted round his neck.

Two night porters in front of a background of white, tense faces of disturbed hotel guests, stared into the room.

Revel indicated the mute on the floor, who was now beginning to come round. "This man broke in and tried to rob me."

The porters' expressions became horrified. An attempted robbery in one of the two four-star hotels in Lyons! *Incroyable!* Reinforced by two more members of the night staff, they bounced into the room and dragged the mute to his feet. An under-manager had by now arrived with a policeman.

In the welter of gesticulating arms and milling bodies, all trying to press into the room to get a close view of the scene of the crime and the criminal, Revel gathered his things and slipped away. He took the lift to the foyer, walked round to the hotel garage, started his hired car, and drove away. It would have been most inconvenient for him to have been delayed by the due processes of French law.

On the outskirts of Lyons on the road back to the north, Revel turned off into a lane leading deep into the heart of one of the vineyards. By the light of his torch he examined the contents of the mute's pockets.

Revel reckoned that when Flek sprang his trap, he would be there or close by, to see that Revel had fallen well and truly into it. He would not leave the final arrangements in the hands of a mute, whose main attributes would appear to have been silence and strength. Therefore the mute, expendable as was the man left behind at Boyard's House, was another sign on the trail. As he couldn't speak, Flek must have seen to it that somewhere on him would be a clue telling Revel where he was to go next. How Flek had so quickly discovered at which hotel Revel had booked, was not just now important.

Revel found the clue in the cheap imitation leather wallet he had taken from the mute's inside jacket pocket. A piece of paper which merely said, " Villa Olga Regina, Cernobbio, Lago di Como. D.F."

Revel thought the initials were a sweet touch, and he sat looking at the piece of paper long after its significance had burnt itself into his mind.

A villa in a little village on the shores of Lake Como in northern Italy—that was the next stop, then. But why? What was the purpose of luring him half-way across Europe when any attempt to kill him could have been made anywhere along the route, thus saving time and trouble? Some sort of attempt had indeed been made a few moments after they had met for the first time. Revel could not believe that because of the failure of that attempt Flek had taken to his heels.

Now Revel was becoming convinced that

it was not only his death Flek sought, but something else besides; but what?

As for his own task—well, it would be just as easy to eliminate Flek in Italy as anywhere else. Or just as deadly.

Chapter Six

THE WATERS of the lake were still, forming a liquid mirror that reflected the mountain slopes swooping skywards from its very edge, and the blue of space spreading to infinity above them.

In the town of Como itself, Revel stood near the water's edge and looked across the narrow strip of the lake towards the village of Cernobbio, dominated by its yellow-wash church. A little to the north of the village, right on the shore of the lake, stood the imposing, historic Villa d'Este, and somewhere about a mile to the north of that, among the trees fringing the lake, stood the Villa Olga Regina. This much Revel had discovered from the waiter who had served his breakfast in the small hotel near the funicular railway, at which he had arrived late the night before.

It was thirty hours since Revel had left Lyons, crossing the Alps and the frontier at Briançon, and sweeping across the wide *autostradi* of northern Italy. Now, the bell in the campanile behind him was striking ten o'clock.

He walked away from the water's edge, back to the table outside the small café where a waiter had already served him with strong, black coffee. He had had only three hours' sleep, but despite his killing drive and lack of rest, his brain was alert, his body keyed to a pitch of fitness and readiness for what lay ahead.

He was clear in his mind as to what he must do. The Villa Olga Regina was almost certainly the place where Flek would spring his trap—in the house itself, or somewhere nearby. But before Flek could spring his trap, Revel must get to Flek, and carry out the order Makepeace had given him. The operative word was "surprise". How to accomplish it was what occupied his mind now.

Fifteen minutes later, in search of a way to surprise Flek, Revel was driving along the lakeside road between Cernobbio and Menaggio. He passed the gateway leading to the grounds in which the Villa Olga Regina stood—the two stone pillars on either side of the innocent-looking open gates, bearing the name of the house on them. It was in a lonely situation. The grounds were surrounded on three sides by the trees which spilled over from the vast wood covering the lower slopes of Monte Bisbino, right down to the lakeside. The lake itself formed the fourth boundary.

Not quite half-way between Cernobbio and Menaggio, Revel turned off left, on to a narrow track which climbed the broad hump of Bisbino towards the nearby Swiss frontier. At the first small house he came to he stopped, and found himself in luck—the man of the house was at home. Revel spoke to the man—a forester who tended the coniferous timber plantations covering the Italian side of the mountain. After several minutes' talking, Revel handed over a quantity of thousand lire notes.

When he left the small house, he left the man and his wife bright-eyed and with more money than they had ever had at any one time in their lives—and poorer by a set of the man's working clothes.

Ten minutes later, a well-built, grimy-faced forester was making a detailed inspection of the trees bordering the low-walled grounds of the Villa Olga Regina.

The fact that the forester quite often seemed to be peering through a heavy cigarette case held in a lengthwise position would have surprised any who saw him. They would have been even more surprised had they been allowed to peer at the Villa through the cigarette case; prisms and an infra-red attachment turned the cigarette case into binoculars which could see right into any room. They cut out any loss of vision due to reflections on the glass of windows, and nullified the darkness of any unlighted interior looked into from outside in daylight. It was a pity, Revel had often thought, that the infra-red ray was not able to pierce brick walls.

Two hours later the forester walked some distance along the road, to where a Mercedes was hidden amongst the thick undergrowth. After ten minutes the car emerged on to the road with Revel at the wheel and a pile of forester's clothing on the floor in the back. Not far from the Villa he left the car, hidden once again, but this time not too cleverly, and returned to Cernobbio on foot. Here he caught the autobus back to Como.

During his inspection of the trees he had seen Flek, the man Saul, and four or five other men moving about in various downstairs rooms. He had also seen the white Mercedes parked on the wide drive-way near the main entrance to the villa. So far as he could see, the place was guarded in no special way, but was the replica of a dozen similar villas in the area—the abodes of well-to-do Italians who had business connections in busy, industrial Milan.

From the trees on a small promontory near the edge of the water, he had been able to study the side of the house facing the lake. And he had seen the trim launch moored to a rickety landing stage built over the rocky shore.

Back in his room at the small hotel near the funicular railway in Como, Revel drew a complete plan of the grounds, the shape of the house, the shape and comparative sizes of the ground floor rooms, the positions of windows and doors. Again and again he drew the same plan until it was burned into his mind foot by foot, so that he would have been able to traverse blindfold his planned approach through the grounds to the villa.

Lunch, a siesta and then, as evening approached, Revel took a taxi to Como's neighbouring lakeside town of Bellaggio directly opposite the grounds of the Villa Olga Regina on the other side of the lake. From a pleasure-craft boatman, he hired a skiff for two days.

Having settled this he took up the old Italian occupation of sitting at an outside café table to watch the world go by. The night was warm and Revel was hot, but he did not remove his jacket as most of the men who strolled past him had done.

Full darkness came and pin-points of light shone on the other side of the lake half a mile away. Lights from the town and waterside restaurants and villas of Bellaggio spilled on to the surface of the lake for a few yards from the shore; beyond was a black back-cloth pricked only occasionally by a flickering dot of light.

Revel went to his hired skiff and joined others who were rowing lazily near the shore —holidaymakers for the most part, enjoying the night-time coolness of the lake. He edged out of the spill-light, then sculled leisurely into the blackness towards a small cluster of lights which he knew to belong to the Villa Olga Regina.

Twenty yards from the rocky end of the villa's garden, he stopped rowing. The windows of the house were another twenty yards beyond the edge of the garden. The lights were on, the french windows wide open after the heat of the day. In the big room, a part of which was plainly disclosed through the open windows, he saw two men moving about then settle down in chairs out of sight.

From specially sewn pockets in the lining of his jacket, Revel took slim, feather-light metal tubes which he proceeded to fit together. The last two attachments to be fitted were a twelve inch, heavier metal tube and a slim four-inch telescopic sight which clicked into position on the last tube. When he had finished he had a light, mini repeating rifle in his hands. He loaded the magazine, and sat in the darkness on the still water—and waited.

For over an hour he sat there, cushioned

by water without currents, before he saw Flek enter the room. The huge man stood for a moment, framed in the lighted window, before passing from view. A second or so later he reappeared, and sat down in a chair, his head and shoulders clearly visible.

Slit-mouthed and cold-eyed, Revel brought the mini-rifle slowly to his shoulder. Just as he was about to take aim through the telescopic sight, the two men he had seen earlier came between him and his target. They half-bent over Flek, and appeared to be sharing a joke. Revel could see their movements and gestures, but could not hear their voices.

He cursed them and wished them a thousand miles away. After a few moments one of the men, still laughing, left the room, while the other seated himself in a chair about a yard from where Flek sat.

Once more Revel took aim, the hair-wires of the sight crossing in the centre of Flek's right temple. Revel steadied, held his breath, and then squeezed the trigger.

The butt of the firmly held gun jarred back into his shoulder. There was the plunk of a silenced explosion, and a semi-suppressed flash spurted from the muzzle. The bullet hammered home dead on target and Flek's body keeled over the side of the chair.

The other man in the room stood up suddenly. He shouted, and then ran for the door, still shouting.

The next second the house became alive. Lights came on in darkened rooms, and now Revel could hear shouting. Half-a-dozen men ran out of the house and sped towards the launch Revel had seen earlier.

Revel was already rowing towards the shore which the launch would shortly leave; but he was aiming to hit land some seventy yards south of the landing stage.

The launch hummed out towards the middle of the lake as Revel pulled the last few strokes. The nose of the skiff grated gently against the rocky shore and he clambered out, securing the boat to a bush some six yards farther inshore.

Then as fast as he could in the darkness, Revel scrambled towards the lights of the villa. He had seen the result of the bullet hitting home. He had been on target. But when he reported to Makepeace, he would have to be able to say that Flek was dead. And he could not be one hundred per cent sure until he had seen the body at close quarters. Ninety-nine point nine per cent would not do.

It would need only a second's glance for him to be one hundred per cent sure. The villa and the grounds looked deserted, and Revel grinned without mirth. The success of the attack on Flek had set the rest of his entourage by the ears. They had been so sure that the shot had come from the lake. . . . And so it had. . . . And he had seen six or seven of them clamber aboard the launch to scour the dark lake for the killer. Flek had suddenly left them, and they were like a snake that has been decapitated, the remainder of its body writhing and twisting without purpose or direction for the short while before that, too, became everlastingly still.

Revel vaulted the low wall and ran towards the still open french windows, from which the light spilled generously.

He held the rifle in his hands, and if there were still one or two of Flek's men in the house. . . .

He edged along the wall of the villa to the open windows. Still there was no sign of movement inside or outside the house—only the steady hum of the launch somewhere out on the lake.

Revel stepped to the threshold of the room, tense, the rifle held in readiness.

There was the chair Flek had been seated in, overturned by the weight of the immense body as it was flung sideways by the impact of the bullet. And near it, Revel could see the shoe-clad feet and trousered legs of the man he had been sent to execute.

He was about to take the few steps that would confirm for ever that Flek was no longer a danger to the nation, when he felt a vicious prod against his spine half-way up his back. In the same breathless, numbed moment, a voice behind him said, " Don't go any farther, Mr. Revel. In fact—don't even move an eyebrow. Saul can't possibly miss at the range from which he will fire."

Revel felt as if his blood had curdled into mud, and all over his body he felt the sharp tingling of shock and panic.

For the voice that had spoken was the mellifluous voice of Damien Flek, the man into whose head Revel had just hammered a hole as big as his fist.

Chapter Seven

THE ROOM was small. It had a door but no windows. It must have had some form of ventilation, probably a vent in the ceiling. But Revel could not be sure about this, for the room was in complete darkness. The little he had learned about it had come from his questing fingers as he felt his way round the room.

The floor and walls—even the door—were padded. There was no furniture, not even a pallet of straw.

This was where he had been flung before the tingling shock of his capture had left him. Six men had been behind him, with the far-from-dead Flek, and once he had been disarmed, four more had appeared through the doorway of the room. This meant that with the five or six who had played out the little scene with the launch, Flek had at least sixteen men in the villa.

As they dragged Revel away, Flek had looked down at the dummy of himself lying on the floor, its head shattered. Before Revel was pulled through the door of the room, Flek had drenched him in his benign smile and had said, " What a pity you don't play on our team, Mr. Revel. You really are quite an accurate shot."

They had taken his jacket, shoes and socks from him, and had removed every other item of equipment he had on him, even his tie, before flinging him into the padded cell.

Revel sat on the floor, his back to the wall, and shrugged; it was useless telling himself now that he should have been expecting something like this—that he should have waited longer before confirming that Flek was dead. It had been obvious from the beginning that Flek was setting a trap for him; with all that his observations had told him, Revel should have known that Flek must be working some sort of double bluff. But what else could he have done?

Revel smiled wryly in the blackness. He knew now what he should have done; he should have played the waiting game—kept Flek on tenterhooks and perhaps have taken more trouble to check on the number of men in the villa; have given Flek time to show what direction the double bluff would take. He should have . . .

A glaring, naked light bulb in the ceiling suddenly blazed into life, bringing a rush of water to his eyes, which he covered protectively with his hands.

"Weeping, Mr. Revel? Surely not."

He looked up at the sound of the voice, shading his streaming eyes with his hand. There had been no noise as the padded door opened, no sound to tell him that it was being opened. Flek stood there, and with him was the cold-eyed Saul, a heavy automatic in his right hand.

The smile on the huge man's face was almost sympathetic. "You must not feel badly about falling into my little trap. Had I been in your position, I might just have been deceived in the same way."

"Where are your troupe of actors performing next, Flek?"

"They *were* rather good, weren't they? The two men who set the dummy in the chair—right under your nose as it turned out—while I crawled away out of sight . . . And did you savour the note of panic the others put into their movements once they

He looked up at the sound of the voice . . .

had learned of the death of their leader? I was touched. It was almost as if they meant it."

Four men came into the room, the door of which had been left open. Two of them carried upright chairs, the third a small, folding card-table, and the fourth carried a tray on which there were two glasses and a bottle of wine. They set up the table and chairs, set the wine on the table, and left the room, shutting the door behind them.

Saul stationed himself and his large automatic in a corner of the room, while Flek seated himself in one of the chairs at the table, and indicated that Revel should seat himself in the other.

"Come, Mr. Revel—join me in a glass of wine. Having succeeded in ... er ... obtaining your presence, I feel like celebrating."

"This seat does me very well. I can fall no lower."

Flek smiled and poured two glasses of wine. "You don't lose gracefully, Mr. Revel."

"Until I'm dead I haven't lost. And anyway, our business isn't a graceful one."

The big man sipped his wine. "Delightful. Do try some. No? You don't think our business is a graceful one? I'm surprised. True, getting you to follow me here needed no finesse at all, seeing that you had orders to hunt me down for elimination purposes. But once I had shown you where I was, and had demonstrated by masterly inactivity how vulnerable both the Villa Olga Regina and I were to a determined man, do you not think the mode of your defeat displayed not only finesse, but a certain grace?"

"I'd have called it low cunning."

"Sour grapes, Mr. Revel, sour grapes."

"From the casual way you laid your trail, I guessed you knew I had orders for your elimination, and that no matter what, I'd dog your footsteps. And of course there were the two expendable characters you used to make sure I wouldn't miss my way."

"Ah, yes. Lazlo and Frangoyannis. We shall miss them—but not much."

"I should have thought you would miss the mute a great deal. He managed to tail me all the way to Lyons without my spotting him. An achievement."

Flek laughed. "But he didn't tail you,

my dear fellow. He was *waiting* for you. Oh, no—we didn't *know* you would book in at the Hotel Royal. But after all, there are only two four-star hotels in Lyons, and nine three-star. And, although we had scarcely met, I knew enough about you to guess that it would be at one of those you would stay. It meant merely the stationing of eleven men—one at each hotel and all expendable, as you say—to await your arrival. Once you had arrived, well, they had their orders not to hurt you too much, and to allow you to extract the information as to my destination from them. We have to keep up appearances, don't we? And it was here I wanted you."

He poured himself another glass of wine. "Are you sure you won't join me? You look so uncomfortable huddled up in that corner on the floor. Still no? Well, please yourself."

"If you wanted to prevent me from killing you, you made a mistake in not eliminating me *en route*. For if I get the opportunity, I shall carry out my orders."

Flek smiled down at Revel. "My dear Mr. Revel, don't be so melodramatic. The slightest move on your part towards violence, and we may *have* to kill you. And that would disappoint me a great deal, for you see, I have other plans for you." He sipped his wine, replaced the glass on the table, spread his huge, fleshy hands on the table top, and leaned forward. "Did you know I have two of your colleagues here, in this house?"

Revel's expression did not alter, but he was shocked at the news—if it were true.

"Oh, it's true enough. And like yourself, they are among the top echelon of the operatives Makepeace employs."

It was a bigger shock to Revel to learn that Flek actually knew the name of Britain's most secret man. Apart from anything else, this alone merited elimination.

He said, "You seem to be singularly well-informed."

"Oh, I am, Mr. Revel, I am. And through you and your two colleagues—oh, by the way, you've guessed who they are of course? Smailey and Drebner?" Flek's smile broadened. "Together they sound like a firm of solicitors, do they not? However, as I was saying, through you and your two colleagues, I shall become even more well-informed. In fact, only a fortnight ago, your Mr. Smailey was good enough to let me have a list of the top radio wavelengths used by the Department, as well as the name of the man who pulls the strings. That's how I learned of your mission to kill me. Merely by listening in to your conversation with Makepeace the night you visited ... er ... me, after they found poor Brent. Oh, yes, Mr. Smailey was most helpful."

"I don't doubt the refinements of your torture methods would break any man."

Flek looked shocked. "Oh, no, Mr. Revel. No torture, I assure you. Mr. Smailey gave me the information, well, not entirely of his own free will, but he was certainly under not the slightest physical pressure, I do assure you."

Revel had worked with Bob Smailey on three assignments; he knew him for a tough, intelligent and dedicated opponent to all that Flek stood for. Revel liked him, and Smailey returned that liking. He was not the sort of man to crack easily under torture, and no amount of brain-washing would have had any effect on him.

"Let me put your mind at rest, Mr. Revel. Mr. Smailey fell into our hands some four weeks ago. Mr. Drebner we netted shortly before my trip to Jersey to deal with George Brent, whose double cover we had broken, oh, maybe three months ago. Brent had to go because I was reaching the climax of Phase One of my plan. And George, unfortunately for him, was too close to me for your people to have unrestricted . . . er . . . control over him."

Flek shrugged. "But all this is really beside the point. To return to what I was saying. All that has happened to Mr. Smailey, is that he has undergone a slight brain operation, in which—I won't bore you with the technical details—a minute cobalt plate has been attached to that part of the brain which exercises control over the will. Mr. Drebner is shortly to undergo the same operation. Oh, I do assure you that the operations are performed by the best brain surgeon in the world—Professor Igor Mantonowski. You will remember he was the Russian doctor in charge of the medical supervision of the mental reactions of the Soviet Cosmonauts in Space? And you will remember, too, perhaps, that he disappeared from sight—believed in the West to have displeased his masters and to have been removed?"

Flek shook his head. "Professor Mantonowksi removed himself, Mr. Revel. He changed his allegiance, quite voluntarily, from the U.S.S.R. to me. Not for money of course, but because there are a number of experiments the Professor wishes to carry out on live human beings, and even his masters jibbed at what he wanted to do. I, on the other hand, having made contact with him, was able to promise him unlimited scope . . . once he had helped me to achieve my Grand Design."

Revel looked up at the giant. "You're mad, of course."

"Not at all, Mr. Revel. And I take your remark as a compliment, for wasn't the great Galileo Galilei considered mad? Was not Leonardo da Vinci considered unbalanced by many?

"But to return to what I was saying. This minute cobalt plate—it cannot be larger than maybe . . . what? . . . three pin-heads ranged side by side?—which has been attached, for want of a better word, to Mr. Smailey's brain, has rendered him completely subservient to an abnormally high-frequency radio wavelength. When he is spoken to on that wavelength—from as far away as three thousand miles it could be—Mr. Smailey can do nothing but obey; he can do nothing but answer questions put to him, truthfully. Only I know the wavelength. And that is all there is to it. Except—I nearly forgot—that a small injection, given during the operation, renders him entirely forgetful of the events leading up to the operation, and of the operation itself. In short, when we release Mr. Smailey to return to his normal occupation—to work for me, of course—he will appear to be the same as he always has been, even to his closest associates, except that he will be entirely under my control. And he won't even be aware of that."

Flek stood up, his large smile beaming down at Revel. "Now, there is no sign of torture in that, is there? So you see, when your turn comes—as it will very shortly—you have nothing to fear. You won't even remember this delightful conversation we are having."

"You'll never get away with it."

"But my dear Mr. Revel, that's just what they said, in effect, to Galileo, when he told them that the Earth revolved round the Sun, and not the other way round as the ancients had believed. I am already getting away with it. Already I have learned many of your country's top secrets. Through you I shall learn more. I have my organisation at work in your country, and in Europe. My industrial and business concerns have branches in nearly every country in Europe. My fortune is so vast that I could buy up eighty per cent of the Texas oil millionaires —and still have something left over. When I have learned all I can from you, and have returned you to the Department to go on with your work—under my supervision, of course—I shall be able, gradually, to get more and more of your top men under control of the wavelength—your politicians, your military, naval and air chiefs."

"Wild-cat. Pie-in-the-sky."

"You take a lot of convincing. The operation takes but a short time. From the time it starts to the time the subject is on his feet again and normal, is only two to three days. Most of my operatives, both here and elsewhere, are already under the wavelength. So you see, I have already made more than a start."

"A brain operation . . . and the subject can be on his feet again and apparently normal within two or three days? Flek—how does he hide the bandages? How does he explain those away?"

"Really Revel, you underestimate the Professor. To begin with, yes, there were bandages—but he has now brought his technique to such a pitch of perfection, that the operation, to put it in the simplest terms, is little more than a very small puncture at the base of the skull, into which the cobalt plate is inserted. It is then coated in a medical substance of the Professor's concoction, which enables it to adhere to the correct lobe of the brain. The plate, you understand, is sensitised to the high frequency wavelength, and is therefore, as you might say, the control panel by which I operate the . . . er . . . operative."

Flek smiled at his own joke. "After two days, there is no external sign of any operation having taken place. There now, I've been very patient with you. It really will work, Revel. Once I have the whole Department under the wavelength, with all the knowledge it possesses, it will not take very long to put Phase Two of the Grand Design into operation, that is, to gain control of the politicians and Service chiefs.

"Through them I shall gain complete control of Britain. And from there, what? Europe ... America ... the world! I shall control the world!"

"You're mad—completely. You can't fetter the minds of nations in this way! I doubt if you can fetter the mind of *one* man who is determined to resist you."

Flek sighed. "Then I must convince you to the contrary."

He lifted his wrist, to which was attached what appeared to be a wristwatch. He adjusted a small panel on the face of it—and then spoke into it. "Bring in Smailey."

Two minutes later the silent door opened, and Smailey walked in. He seemed in good health, fit, alert; the same fair-haired, wide-shouldered and craggy-faced Smailey that

Revel knew. The good-humour, a foundation of Smailey's pleasing character, was still evident in his eyes.

He saw Revel sitting on the floor, and looked delighted to see him, but not surprised. "Hello, Roy. It's good to see you. But what in the world are you doing down there? No shoes . . . socks. . . ."

Flek, watching the scene with an amused look on his face, adjusted the apparatus at his wrist again, and again spoke into it. "Kill him," he said.

Smailey's expression remained unchanged. Only his attitude altered; his muscles tensed, and his gaze concentrated on Revel's throat. Like a stalking tiger he moved towards his friend, his hands held in front of him, fingers flexed.

And then suddenly he pounced, the fingers of both hands clamped round Revel's neck in a grip of steel. As the pressure increased, he continued to look into Revel's eyes with the same friendly expression he had worn when he had first seen him in the room.

It was horrifying, and completely and utterly unexpected . . . unbelievable. Under the strength of those hands, and the suddenness and shock of the attack, Revel was helpless.

His lungs were bursting, his tongue was becoming too big for his mouth, and the last thing he saw before the thickening red mist in front of his eyes shut out all vision, all feeling, all sensation, was the kindly, craggy face of his friend Smailey—who was concentrating on choking the life out of him.

Chapter Eight

"HE'S NOT DEAD—but he should be. The pressure was maintained too long for safety."

"I let my enthusiasm for the demonstration run away with me. However, he's not dead, so—put him on the wavelength as soon as possible."

"I shall be glad when we have reached Phase Three. I am becoming bored with this . . . I have so much more important work to do . . . so much more of the depths of the human mind to unravel."

"Then, my dear Professor, remember that it is only by doing this work, that you will be able to go further in exploring the mind of man. I'll leave you Praxates and Vilmout to look after the patient until you are ready for him."

A door opened, and then clicked shut.

Revel's mind recorded the conversation it had heard, as well as the opening and shutting of the door. But at that moment it meant nothing to him. It hurt him to swallow and for a fraction of a second he wondered why he had a sore throat.

And then memory came flooding back to him. With it came a great anger at what had been done to Smailey. Suddenly the conversation he had just heard meant something to him. He had been the subject of the conversation, a cold, callous collection of words. Previously, his feeling towards Flek had been quite impersonal; there had been no hate behind what he had been ordered to do. There had been the knowledge that the man was a danger to the life of the nation, so much so that Makepeace had ordered his elimination. But Revel had experienced no personal feeling of loathing for the man he had to kill.

Now he did; now that he had seen what had happened to Smailey, and now that he had heard the conversation about himself, a cold, deadly anger against Flek and everything he stood for, nearly choked him. But he quenched his red-hot anger in icy, calculated thought. His fury must not cloud his brain, must not push him into premature action.

Cautiously he opened his eyes. He was

in what appeared to be a small side-ward of an operating theatre. Clinical, white-glazed tiles covered the walls, and the floor was smooth and polished. There was a glass partition, on the other side of which he could see two masked, white-clad figures standing over an operating table. A fierce arc-light shone down on them. He could not see if there was anyone on the operating table from where he was lying.

On his left, over by the door through which Flek must have just passed, sat two men, well-built, cold-eyed after the pattern of the human misfits Flek had gathered about him. One of them held a weapon loosely in his right hand—not an automatic, Revel decided . . . it must be a spray gun containing some sort of neutralising gas to render him helpless should he prove trouble-some. Flek, having progressed thus far, would almost certainly not want him killed at this stage.

Apart from the narrow, hospital-type bed on which he was lying, and the two chairs on which his guards were seated, Revel could see no other article in the room. There was a window in the wall to his right through which he could see a small patch of blue sky—which meant he had been unconscious for some time—and the branches of a tree, quite close.

He knew the room was on the first floor; he had seen no room fitted like this when he made his observations of the ground-floor rooms, and from the closeness of the tree, he knew he was on the south side of the house. This too, he recalled from his observations. He forced into his mind the details of the plan he had drawn over and over again. Would it be possible. . . .? There was certainly the chance that he might break his neck. . . . But it was, he decided, a case of neck or nothing.

He sat up slowly with a groan. The two men rose from their chairs. One of them called, "Professor!"

Mantonowski came into the room from the theatre, pulling off the linen mask which covered the bottom half of his face. "Ah, he is conscious. Good."

Revel put his feet to the ground with the same slowness, and pushed himself into a standing position, teetering weakly.

"You two—help him into the theatre. It

may be that after his manhandling, he is not yet recovered enough for the operation. I must examine him. The other is under sedation and can wait."

The two men came one on either side of Revel, put their arms round him, supporting him roughly, and flinging his supine arms round their shoulders.

"This one shouldn't give you much trouble, Professor," one of them said.

Mantonowski's smooth face wreathed itself into a smile; behind his thick, pebble-lens glasses, his eyes creased into slits. "Trouble? None of them gives me trouble, once they have felt my little needle. Bring him in."

He turned to lead the way into the operating theatre, where his assistant stood waiting. Even if he had not turned his back it would probably have made no difference, for Revel's anger had increased with his swiftly returning strength. His fury that such men could exist had given him the will to push his strength to the uttermost.

Mantonowski first heard a sound as if two coconuts, full of milk, had been slammed together. Then he felt a terrific blow between his shoulder blades, and was sent stag-

*It sounded as if two coconuts had been
slammed together . . .*

gering forward to crash into the glass partition, through which he tumbled in a shower of glass and splintered wood. He was accompanied by two very unconscious men, whose heads had just been forced together in an unexpected and somewhat violent collision, propelled and encouraged by Revel's arms, which they had themselves obligingly flung round their own necks.

The third stage of the proceedings was again accompanied by the sound of shattering glass, as Revel hurled himself, hunched up, his arms covering his head protectively, through the window.

For a milli-second the hanging branch of the tree swept in front of his eyes; below him the earth was rushing to meet him with a force that would have broken both his legs, and maybe caused him more serious injury.

He flung out his arms, his fingers crooked into desperate hooks. If he missed now, he missed everything.

The harsh bark of the tree tore at the flesh on the palms of his hands, but the waiting, desperate fingers gripped like vices. The falling weight of his body jarred at his shoulder sockets painfully. The branch sagged under his weight, and twigs from other branches whipped him spitefully in the face.

Before the branch recovered to swing upwards again, Revel let go, and dropped the remaining eight feet to the ground. He scarcely felt the pain as his bare feet crashed on the gravel. Dragging himself out of a stagger, he flung himself in the same movement down three stone steps leading to the solid fuel store beneath the ground floor of the villa.

Revel's body bounced against the locked door, which forced a grunt from him. After this he lay there, hunched against the door in the small well at the bottom of the steps. He tried hard not to let the harshness of his breathing be heard. Unless somebody came almost to the edge of the steps, he could not be seen. He hoped too that the recess in which the low door to the fuel store was set, was of sufficient depth for the overhang of the stone lintel to hide him from anyone looking down from an upstairs window.

There was silence for a few moments after

this violent action; then, as on the night when he had shot Flek's dummy, the house came alive.

He heard Flek's voice—no longer mellifluous, but harsh and almost screeching in rage—shout from the front of the house. "Split up, fools! Eight of you to the road—four go north, four south. You three go through the wood to the south of the house —the rest of you search the trees to the north. He can't get far! Get him! Get him, do you hear? And bring him back—alive or dead. But bring him back!"

The sound of running feet . . . and then three men moving fast, came briefly into Revel's vision as they made for the low boundary wall and the trees to the south beyond. The sound of other footsteps running in other directions soon faded.

Revel looked at his bleeding feet, swallowed slowly because of the soreness of his throat, and smiled crookedly and without mirth. Phase One of his own Grand Design had come off—he had temporarily reduced the size of the opposition by a considerable number. But what would Flek do now?

And how many of his men still remained in or near the house?

The smile left his face as he heard the now strangely harsh voice of Flek again. "They'll get him—they'll get him! He can't get far. But just in case he doubles back to try and get at the professor again now that most of us are out searching for him, you Saul, and I, will patrol round the house. You circle that way, I'll go in the opposite direction. Keep close to the wall of the house—it will serve to protect you. If you see him—shoot!"

Revel tensed himself. This was not quite what he had bargained for. Now discovery was only a matter of seconds away. He wondered which of them Fate would send to find him out.

Chapter Nine

REVEL remained frozen in a huddle by the door for only a second longer. Then he sprang from the well between the bottom step and the door, up to ground level. In a stumbling, headlong scramble he reached the corner of the building as steady footsteps crunched on the gravel, coming nearer and nearer. He stopped about two feet back from the angle of the wall, and dropped to a stooping position.

Saul came round the corner of the villa, his face set in the grim, hard expression of the Slav, his eyes moving over the ground ahead. An automatic was held purposefully in his right hand.

It needed split-second timing on Revel's part. His attack had to be restrained until Saul had come round the corner of the building—in case Flek looked back before himself turning the angle of the wall at the other end of the house. But the attack had to be pressed home before Saul, having seen Revel, could bring his gun to bear. And

Saul had to be prevented from shouting or firing a shot that would bring the giant Flek pounding to his aid.

Saul was half-way through his second step past the angle of the house when he saw Revel—and that was a milli-second after Revel had made his movement. By then it was too late for Saul.

Revel flung himself upwards, his left fist ram-rodding into Saul's solar plexus. At the same time, as Saul sagged forward from the force of the blow, his breath coming out like the suppressed wail from a banshee, Revel slashed his right hand down in a sweeping karate blow to the back of the man's neck.

Saul hit the ground face down. The whole operation had taken less than three seconds. It was textbook stuff, and Revel's eyes glinted with satisfaction, his lips spread in a wolfish grin.

Now, suddenly, his mind was crystal clear; he knew exactly what he was going to do—what he *must* do. No longer was he playing each move as Flek called it, by ear; for the first time *he* was calling the tune.

He felt the headlong, joyous disregard for

himself, for everyone and everything that always came to him in the midst of action. Now he was a ruthless machine, powered by steel-like sinews, controlled by a cool mind, inspired by a heart and will which only death could break.

He scooped up the automatic from where it had fallen on the gravel, and ran round to the main entrance of the villa. He bounded up the steps and into the tiled hall. There was a man there, part of the remnant of the force Flek had left as rear-guard inside the house itself.

His jaw dropped as he saw the human tornado whirling towards him, felt the force of a punch that almost separated his skull from his spinal column, broke four of his teeth, and rendered him suddenly and deeply unconscious.

The thickly carpeted stairs were balm to Revel's lacerated feet. He had a good idea of the location of the operating theatre, and at the head of the stairs he turned left in the wide corridor, heading for a set of double doors facing him at the far end.

By now Flek must have discovered the body of Saul, and would probably be speaking into his wrist transmitter, recalling his men.

Revel had no time to see if the double doors were locked, or merely shut. He built up his speed along the corridor, and at the end hurled his whole travelling weight, shoulder first, at the white-painted doors.

They splintered open, swinging back violently, and hammering against the walls of the small foyer formed by a glass partition. Beyond was the operating theatre. To the right was a door which must have led into the side-ward attached to the theatre.

Mantonowski's assistant, a youngish, thin-faced, staring-eyed man had the misfortune to be in the foyer. One swinging door, like a beating wing of doom, slapped cruelly into him, and he fell back with a moan against the partition. With his hands over his bleeding face, he slid to the floor.

Revel controlled the staggering rush with which he entered the foyer, and dragged the man to his feet by the lapels of his white, medical jacket. The hands came tremblingly away from the swollen features. There was fear and panic in the man's eyes, which

Revel's devil grin did nothing to mitigate. He swung the man round, and flung him like a sack into the corridor. The assistant slithered for some yards, and then, moaning in fear, he stumbled and scrambled to the head of the stairway in a desperate attempt to escape the death he was sure was close behind him.

In the operating theatre Mantonowski, startled by the crashing doors and the thump and rattle of the partition, came to the doorway, a linen mask over the lower half of his face, his eyes wide behind the pebble-lenses. There was a cut on his nose, one of many received only a few minutes before, after his own more forceful collision with the other glass partition separating the operating room from the side-ward. In his rubber-gloved hand he held a surgeon's knife, with a peculiar, paper-thin attachment a quarter of the way up the blade.

He was frightened, but there was more backbone in him than in his assistant. He raised the knife and slashed at Revel's face with a strangely awkward movement for one to whom a scalpel was a daily tool.

Revel grinned viciously as he easily evaded the slash, and hammered his fist into the white mask. The professor's glasses flew from his face as his head was jerked back; the scalpel dropped from his hand, and he himself matched the speed with which it fell to the floor.

On the operating table was the figure of a man lying face down. It was Drebner, and Revel hoped he was in time to stop Mantonowski starting the operation.

He had no time to find out. Flek stood in the doorway of the theatre, an automatic aimed directly at Revel. But it was deadlock, for Revel was facing the door, and his automatic had been aimed at the opening which Flek filled.

The benign, drenching smile had now been wiped from Flek's face. Fury and all the evil in the man twisted and writhed over his round, fleshy features. His lips were creased back from his teeth in a purely animal snarl, and his eyes stabbed into Revel like the flickering fangs of a poisonous reptile.

The sight of this giant manifestation of

evil was all that was needed to feed the white-hot fire of Revel's anger, to keep up the terrific momentum of his attack.

It was as if, for these two, the impersonal exchange of bullets from a distance was not enough. Only a physical, hand-to-hand battle to the death would satisfy either.

Their weapons hit the floor almost at the same time, as they allowed them to fall from their hands. It was a silent, deadly agreement, inspired by such a depth of hate as only close combat could quench.

They were separated by four yards, and their eyes held each other, waiting for the move that must end—for one of them—in the everlasting stillness of death.

Chapter Ten

THE MOVE came from Flek—a slow, gorilla-like movement that brought him to within arm's distance of Revel, who was standing half-crouched, every sinew in his body tensed.

Flek was taller, more thickly built, and considerably heavier. Revel knew there would be no holds barred; feet, hands, heads, knees—these were all to be used. And perhaps any small weapon that Flek still had on him; this was something to be ready for.

Flek took a lightning step forward, and his huge arms wrapped round Revel like two huge metal clamps. And then he used his weight, forcing Revel back until he was bent like a bow.

Revel butted his head forward with all the strength he could muster. He brought both feet up off the ground, swung them high, as if he were trying to somersault backwards, and then hammered his heels into Flek's face, which, a moment before, had taken the full force of Revel's hard skull.

The big man's hold weakened momentarily, long enough for Revel to force his imprisoned arms free and complete the somersault, using his bare heels, pressed against the giant's face as his starting block.

He landed on all fours, facing his enemy whose nose was spread over the centre of his face. Flek, his eyes blazing, crouched over him, his right hand stiff and flexed, ready to smash down on the side of Revel's neck. Revel's eyes flicked to the big man's stomach, and Flek shifted his hand slightly in a protective movement. Revel flung himself at the enormous hand, grasping the wrist in both of his, lifting it violently, before turning his whole body suddenly, and bringing the wrist down with a whirling force.

Flek's huge bulk left the floor; his feet came up and his head dipped. He crashed on his back a few inches from where Mantonowski still lay. But like an enormous conger eel, he rolled and undulated at terrific speed clear of Revel's pounce, and scythed the back of his hand against the side of his enemy's face.

The blow sent the Englishman reeling against the already shattered glass partition, and both men had time to get to their feet and confront each other in the same crouching, tiger-like positions they were in at the start. Revel's head was singing, and his limbs took that fraction of a second longer to obey his will. He stalled for time, backing slowly until his head cleared.

Flek sensed he had shaken his man, and came forward aggressively to use his advantages of height, weight and build in the back-breaking bear hug he had used before. This time he would be ready for Revel's tactics, and this time the Englishman would not escape from his hold.

Revel knew that the bear hug was his greatest danger. He must keep from getting in too close. As Flek came at him, Revel made as if to retreat, so that Flek increased the tempo of his advance. Then as Flek was in the middle of an advancing step, Revel flung himself forward, thrusting his fist out at the same time. Behind the blow was the strength of his arm, the forward hammering of the arm itself, and the hurling movement of his whole body.

His fist sank into Flek's stomach like a stake being driven into soft earth. The breath came out of the giant like a grampus blowing. Blood drained from his face, and his aggressive advance became a staggering lurch.

But even then, while his huge carcase was fighting agonisingly for breath, he brought up his hands to cushion the blow aimed at the side of his jaw, and his fingers closed over Revel's forearm as it plunged forward. He gathered all his remaining strength to use the forearm like the handle of a whip, to crack Revel's body forward so that it sailed over his own slowly sagging trunk.

Revel hit the long-suffering partition, and dropped heavily on to Mantonowski, who had begun to show signs of coming round. Revel's falling weight knocked the senses from him again. Miraculously neither of the men had come into contact with the operating table on which the unconscious form of Drebner still lay.

Flek was on all fours, gasping like a goldfish whose bowl has been smashed. Desperately he tried to get his numbed respiratory organs to work. Revel dragged himself to his feet, forced the muzziness from his brain and made for the gasping gargantuan man.

Flek forced his drooping head up, his mouth a wide air vent. Revel hit him then with all his strength. The blow landed on the side of the jaw, and the skin on Revel's knuckles broke. The big man sagged. Revel hit him again and Flek keeled over heavily, like a stunned bull.

Revel stood over him, panting. He went to Mantonowski, who was coming round again, stripped his white jacket from him, and ripped it into narrow lengths. Within four minutes Flek was bound hand and foot, and Revel leaned against the partition waiting for him to come round.

Mantonowski started to get to his feet, reminding Revel that he was still a potential danger. With the remaining strips of his own jacket, the professor allowed himself to be bound.

It crossed Revel's mind that if Flek had sent out the recall to his men when he found Saul's body, most of them should have returned by now. But as yet, there was no sign that they had.

Revel removed the transmitter from Flek's wrist; it looked as though it were undamaged. The big man stirred and his eyes, flecked with red, animal anger, looked up at his enemy.

Revel said, "I was going to kill you, Flek. But another thought struck me. You're going to tell me the controlling wavelength. I'll even make a bargain with you. The wavelength in return for four hours' start before I set out to hunt you down again."

"Never," Flek spat up at him.

"If you don't give it to me, then I shall kill you—now."

"Then kill me. Do anything. Tear me to pieces while I'm still alive, and you still won't get the wavelength from me."

The hate, the fury, the madness. . . . Suddenly Revel knew that Flek meant every word he said. He would suffer torture, die, but his distorted brain would never allow him to divulge the wavelength. Revel shrugged. Somehow, perhaps, the Department with their scientific aids would be able to discover it—in time. Meanwhile, how much more damage could be done to the nation?

And then the idea came to him. It was so blazingly simple, so apt, so just . . . so *right*!

He went to Mantonowski, dragged him into the side-ward, and then lifted him on to the narrow bed. He stood over him, and the short-sighted eyes looked up at him in stark fear.

Revel found the scalpel and the pebble-lensed glasses among the debris littering the theatre floor. He carried them back into the side-ward.

It took him just two minutes to persuade the professor to do what he demanded. Mantonowski had a deadly fear of the surgeon's knife, which he had daily used on others with such callous indifference. Revel held it to the base of his skull. " I suppose I could just about manage not to kill you, but to so damage your brain that for the rest of your life you would be nothing but a gibbering imbecile. On the other hand, if you do as I say . . ."

It was enough. Mantonowski himself

helped to lift the unconscious body of Drebner into the side-ward. Then he took a
syringe and stood trembling over the prone
figure of Flek, who at first did not understand
what was to happen. As soon as he saw the
syringe, however, fear leapt into those hot,
animal eyes.

"No! No!"

And then the needle sank into the flesh on
the underside of his forearm.

With difficulty they lifted the unconscious
bulk on to the operating table. Revel wheeled
in the trolley containing the surgical instru-
ments. He grinned at the professor, and
bowed ironically.

"Now play, Professor, play," he said.

He picked up the two automatics from
the floor. "A bullet from one of these, properly aimed, can be most painful, Professor.
Don't try any tricks." Then he closed the
double doors of the foyer and piled the
scanty furniture from the side-ward against
them, to keep them shut. They would stand
a certain amount of force before giving way.

He interrupted Mantonowski's prepara-
tions to make the professor show him the
way to the kitchen stores. Between them they

collected tinned food, bread and coffee, and returned to the theatre. Water was laid on in the operating room itself. Revel checked that the door of the side-ward leading into the foyer was locked, and then returned once more to the operating theatre. Now, with a slight barrier between him and Flek's returning men, and with Flek himself as a hostage, Revel felt he could withstand a two-day siege.

As he watched Mantonowski work on Flek, he wondered where Smailey was held in the villa. There had been no time to search for him, but he reckoned that Smailey would be able to survive for up to two days if necessary. . . .

Within the next five minutes Flek's men began drifting back. Flek had not sent out a return call, then. Revel grinned. It was the key action Flek had forgotten in his blind hate and anger.

From the shattered window of the side-ward Revel told them what had happened. The two automatics which he had trained on them, prevented the men from rushing up to overwhelm him by sheer weight of numbers.

To prove to them that he had Flek in his control, he showed them the transmitter.

"The slightest attempt on the part of any one of you to approach this part of the house will mean your leader's death. Keep away until further orders. He dies if one of you makes a move in this direction. Understood?"

They understood that much. What they could not understand was how Revel had so completely turned the tables; without the controlling voice on the wavelength, they were like ships without power, without rudders; they drifted . . . and did nothing. . . .

By evening the professor had completed the major part of the operation; the minute cobalt plate was in position on the brain. Now there was a five-hour wait to ensure that the plate had become firmly attached to the lobe.

By evening too, Drebner, on whom Mantonowski had not had time to operate, had come round. But he must have had an allergy to the anaesthetic used on him, for he remained weak and sick, unable for the time being to stand without support. Revel made him comfortable in the side-ward.

Midnight passed, and Mantonowski, checking, reported the operation on Flek complete and successful. Now there was a further wait of between two to four hours for him to regain consciousness.

Revel spent the time studying the watch-like transmitter. In place of the watch face, there was a lace-like grill into which he had seen Flek speak. Around the rim there was a serrated ring, which he had seen Flek move. Just inside this, on the immovable face, were small marks like the minute marks on the dial of a clock.

Very gingerly Revel exerted a slight clockwise pressure on the ring. It remained firm. He tried in an anti-clockwise direction, and now the ring moved through about four degrees before clicking into a stop-position. So far as Revel could remember, Flek had made only one small adjustment before speaking into the transmitter. There appeared to be no other external, movable parts.

Revel breathed deeply, strapped the transmitter to his wrist, and waited. On this hung the final success or failure of his plan.

As dawn made the sky grey, Flek stirred.

Mantonowski was a spent force. He sat huddled on the floor in a corner of the room, his head bowed.

Revel walked from the window where he had kept vigil and stood looking down at the supine giant. Flek's eyes gazed up at him, vacant at first, but as recognition dawned, all the anger and hate he had ever shown blazed in them. He made a futile effort to free himself from the bonds that still held him captive.

Revel lifted the transmitter to his mouth, his eyes on Flek, his pulses pounding. Now he would know if his guesswork had been right. Now he would know if his victory was a knock-out, or merely a win on points.

Flek mouthed in fury. " I shall get out of this, Revel, and I shall kill you. You'll die the slowest and most painful death I can devise ! "

Revel spoke into the transmitter. " Flek! Instruct all your operatives everywhere to give themselves up at the nearest police station, giving the police the full story of their activities."

The rage in Flek's eyes did not abate, the hatred in them still burned, but he im-

His eyes blazed with rage . . .

mediately began speaking into the transmitter which Revel held close to his mouth.

"All operatives in Sections One to Five, report to the nearest police station. Reveal to the police the full story of your activities."

The rage-filled eyes were turned to Revel. "You'll have to adjust the control-band a single move anti-clockwise."

Revel did so.

Flek spoke into the transmitter again. "All executive personnel in Groups A to F report to the nearest police station. Reveal to the police the full story of your activities. That is all."

Revel said, "You have spoken to every man—and woman—in your organisation?"

"Every one."

Revel heard footsteps outside on the gravel. He went to the window. Flek's men were walking out of the villa towards the road; they walked in a body, silent, and with a definite purpose.

Revel turned, grinning at the hate-twisted face of Flek. "It looks as if you have done just that, my friend," he said.

For the next hour Revel was busy in the

house. He found the rest of his clothes and all his equipment in a room Flek obviously used as an office. He spoke to the Department on his mini-radio; he found Smailey sitting comfortably and undisturbed in a sort of bed-sitting room on the first floor at the other end of the house.

Smailey's robust mentality withstood quite well the shock of what Revel had to tell him.

By that afternoon other Department men had arrived by air from London to take over Flek and Mantonowski, and Revel, Smailey and Drebner were on a Department plane on their way to London, having boarded the aircraft at Milan airport.

In the plane Revel removed his shoes, giving a sigh of relief as the restricting leather came away from his cut and bruised feet. Smailey and Drebner looked at him with raised eyebrows.

Revel said, " There's only one thing about this job of ours—it's killing on the feet."

The following day Revel was in the office above the jeweller's shop near Lansdowne Square. Makepeace, from behind a pile of newspapers on his desk, grinned over at him.

The headlines, most of them shock-streamers, shouted, "Spy ring smashed. . . ." "Astounding success for Britain's Secret Service." "Europe-wide Anarchist Organisation Destroyed " . . . "The Secret Men of Britain Keep Silent on Brilliant Success."

"Not a bad job, not bad at all," said Makepeace. "I suppose you'll want some leave now?"

"Well, I was hoping . . ."

"It was a pity, of course, that they allowed Flek to surprise them and fling himself out of the aircraft which was bringing him here. There'll be an inquiry of course, and someone's head will roll. Still, the Alps are nasty things to fall on from fifteen thousand feet —especially if you have no parachute. You've completed your report, I suppose?"

"Yes. I was hoping . . ."

"It seems that they can remove that plate from Smailey's skull without too much trouble. Now about that leave of yours . . ."

"Well, I was planning . . ."

"I'm afraid you'll have to take a rain check on it. You see there's this fellow in Zambia . . . building up a terrific terrorist organisation, and no one knows who he is—except that they call him the Kalmooza. Inspired by the other side, of course. Now, there's a plane ready for you at Gatwick. I'll give you all we know about things at the moment. . . ."